THE DOG
WHO COULD SPEAK
CAT

THE DOG
WHO COULD SPEAK
CAT

By

Nuala Willis

Drawings
by
Robin Archer

Nuala Willis

Robin Archer

Lulu

2014

For
Miss Toast
and her devoted companion Melinda Patton

&
We'd like to thank our good friends,
Karen Wallis and Robert Gay who helped to launch this project.

Hi there!
Glad you've opened this book.
It's mine. I mean I wrote it.

My name is Miss Toast. That's me at the computer. And this story is from my Dog Blog. You probably don't speak Dog, so I've put it in this book for you.

Before I start I should tell you a bit about myself. I live at Bed 'N Bones, the popular Bed & Breakfast place for dogs, where I assist Slippers who's the owner and my best friend.

When I say assist, well, I do what I can. Pugs have short legs, so I can't do much more than look busy, welcome the guests, keep the peace, that sort of thing. Slippers does the rest, because she can.

I call her Slippers because that's what she wears. We dogs always look at faces first to see if they're friendly. Then we sniff the shoes, you can tell a lot from a pair of shoes. And so that's how we name people.

We're in a quiet street not far from the middle of a big city and we get lots of guests. Some dogs just stay till teatime, some overnight, and some for ages. There are lots of regulars who've become friends, like Teddy and Vero and some regulars like Gertrude, who's a pug like me. She can be fun, but she's mostly big trouble and can make my life real hell.

I call them The Bones Gang, and thanks to Slippers always having her laptop close to hand, I post our adventures in my blog, duties allowing!

(Slippers doesn't know I do this, so it's our secret!)

This adventure happened last Spring and it still makes my fur stand on end to think about it. It all started as the dogs were going home at the end of the week....................

BLOG POST

Trees are green again and it's warm but the wind whips suddenly round corners blowing dust in your eyes. Not good for pugs, as you dogs out there will know, we have big, bulgy eyes.

I chased the cat at Number 32 today. He was very insulting about my figure, at least I think he was. My understanding of Cat is not very good, but I could tell by the sneer on his face that he wasn't flattering me.

Cats are such a pain, why do they think they're better than us dogs?

Big rumpus going on here at Bed 'N Bones. The fizzy feeling in the air, which has made us all feel very bouncy and frisky, seems to have affected Slippers too. She's rushing round the house with mops and brooms, pulling stuff out of the cupboards upstairs and shoving it into big black bags which she takes to a busy shop down the road.

It's huge fun, and as there are only three guests staying at the moment, we can all join in the game. Well, Vero doesn't. He doesn't like games. But Teddy, Gertrude and I love rushing at the mop as it swooshes across the kitchen floor, getting our paws terribly wet. Of course Gertrude, who never knows when to stop, pulled a big chunk out of the mop and covered everyone with water.

Slippers didn't seem to mind too much, in fact she laughed, but when we started grabbing anything she threw towards the black bags and rushing downstairs with it, she wasn't so pleased. Especially when a big woolly cardigan ended up rather the worse for wear. Gertrude again!

Weird that a pug could behave so badly. I could tell Slippers didn't care for our help. She smelt cross, and I don't know what she was saying but she shut us in the sitting room and stamped back upstairs.

We were sitting feeling rather glum when we heard the phone ringing. Slippers stamped back down the stairs. There was silence followed by Slippers yelling in a very angry voice for quite a long time. Teddy pricked up his terrier ears and said to me in a low growl,

"That sounds bad."

The phone was slammed down and we heard Slippers coming toward the sitting room. She flung open the door, red in the face, said something very angry to Gertrude and, muttering to herself, stormed out to the kitchen. We could hear her crashing about as she filled the kettle.

"So what did I do?" Gertrude looked outraged. "How come I always get the blame for everything?"

"Well, you did give that cardigan a hard time," said Teddy, pulling back his lips in a grin.

"So did you. You were growling at that sleeve when you pulled it off."

A thin voice came from behind us. I'd forgotten about Vero (his name is Versace, but I always call him Vero).

"I think," he said from his special chair, "that Slippers planned to go away this weekend, but only with Miss T. Sounds like something might have messed that up."

How does he know these things? He always has the answers. Maybe it's a Chinese Crested thing. That's the breed of dog he is. So maybe they're really smart to make up for how strange they look, being totally bald except for their tails and ears. Is there anyone out there who knows?

Teddy and Gertrude were still squabbling about that wretched cardigan. I snapped at them,

"Oh, stop it you two. I'm going to see what's happening."

So we all trotted into the kitchen. Slippers was staring grumpily out of the window, drinking her coffee and taking big, angry bites out of something soft and sweet. It smelt delicious. She even threw some to us. Really, really unusual.

Finally, she picked up her phone and pressed the little buttons. We could sense she was unhappy. Whoever she was talking to was not happy either. A loud, cross voice was coming out of the phone and Slippers was making 'I'm sorry' noises. Shaking her head, she put down the phone and poured herself another cup of coffee. I looked anxiously at the others.

"What do you think has happened, Teddy?"

"Don't know, but it doesn't feel good," he said watching her eat the last bit of cake. He was drooling. Gertrude snorted.

"Maybe she'll be better now she's had that snack. I could have done with that last bit." She gave a long whine. "Oh! I'm SO bored. I can't wait to go home. Thought Pink Trainers was coming to pick me up today."

"How can you tell?" Teddy looked surprised.

"Well, I usually get a feeling, a kind of sense. You know don't you, Toastie?"

I hate her calling me Toastie, but I wagged my tail in agreement.

"Funny thing though," Gertrude continued, "I'm not feeling it at the moment."

We left the kitchen and curled up quietly in the sitting room. I felt uneasy, so when I heard Slippers go back upstairs I followed. To my surprise she took down her Going-Away-Bag and started filling it with clothes. Is she going away after all? Is she so cross she's going to leave us? Felt even more uneasy. I went gloomily downstairs only to find Gertrude on my pile of cushions! Grrrrrrr!

Afternoon biscuit time

Shiny Shoes came and collected Teddy. I watched him getting into the car. I was sad to see him go. Hope another guest arrives quickly. But nobody came, and finally Very High Heels clicked up the garden path to pick up Vero.

"Good luck, Miss T. I think you're going to need it," he whispered as he picked his way carefully towards the front door. As usual Gertrude had left her toys everywhere.

My tail drooped. It'll be a nightmare being on my own with Gertrude. She ALWAYS sits on my pile of cushions, steals my food and, worse, worms her way onto Slippers' lap.

"Looks like it's just you and me now, old girl," Gertrude said gleefully as we watched Very High Heels drive away.

"Won't that be fun?" I replied sourly.

"I promise not to tease if you stop being a spoil-sport."

On our evening walk we went past the big old Victorian graveyard. It always seems spooky to me. The gates were firmly shut.

"I'd like to go exploring in there, that could be fun. I bet it's stuffed full of foxes," Gertrude said trying to pull Slippers towards the gate so she could look through. Slippers absent-mindedly wandered towards it and Gertrude and I stuck our heads through the bars.

"You don't often see foxes during the day. They like coming out at night, and they're dangerous to us dogs." I hoped I might frighten her a bit. "They're fierce and they don't mind a fight," I added looking at her sideways.

"Neither do I. I'd soon sniff 'em out."

I sighed. This is not going to be an easy few days, or however long she's staying.

Next Breakfast

As we had our noses in our breakfast bowls, Slippers was tidying the kitchen, closing and locking windows, and putting our things in a bag which she left in the hall with her own.

Gertrude looked up from her bowl, which she'd licked clean.

"What's happening? Are we going somewhere?"

"Don't know, Gertie. Maybe we are going away after all. I think Slippers tried to tell me something when I woke up this morning, but I couldn't understand. I gave her a good sniff and she smelt stressed, but kind of excited as well."

The next thing we know we're down the path, out of the gate and into her smelly old car, both of us on a rug on the back seat.

Gertrude started leaping about shouting,

"We're going on a holiday! We're going on a holiday!"

Slippers was just about to put on her seat belt, but she swung round and barked something crossly. To my surprise Gertrude shut up.

We drove for a long time, our faces glued to the windows.

I love being in a car, there's so much to see. Of course

Gertrude yelled at every dog we passed, always stupid comments about how dumb they looked or what weird tails or funny ears they had, or how fat or slow they were. She just can't help it.

Finally, we were driving through a big green space. It looked like Dog Heaven. Loads of trees, no doubt covered in interesting smells. However, nothing could have prepared us for the scent that hit our snouts as minutes later we got out of the car. I went cold, and I could feel the fur along my spine rise in fear. Gertrude turned and looked at me. She was shivering.

"What's that scent? It's like a very big cat. Maybe a lion!"

"Or a tiger," I said.

"There's something else too." Gertrude's eyes widened. "Quite a lot of something else, and whatever it is, it's BIG!"

We looked nervously around us but couldn't see anything. Slippers picked up the bags and off we went. We were heading straight towards whatever it was. We crossed a road, and then a bridge over a small canal. Just the other side of the bridge was a gate with steps going down to the water, and through this gate we went. Soon we were on a narrow path, and close to it in the water were three or four boats like long, low houses. We stopped alongside the third one and Slippers called out.

Almost immediately a door opened and a big woman in old deck shoes came out waving and smiling. She had a nice face. We could tell she liked dogs. Slippers picked me up and put me on the boat. Gertrude scrambled on deck by herself. Then there was a lot of hugging and laughing.

Old Deck Shoes waved us through the door and we found ourselves at the top of some steep, difficult steps that faced a long, low room. We had to get down by jumping onto a small table and then a chair. There was an awful lot of furniture and plants and things hanging down and shiny things on shelves. And running to meet us was a very small Pomeranian dog. He spoke in Dog but with a really strong Cat accent, almost that Meow sound they make. Gertrude was so surprised she just mumbled Hello and stared.

"Oh, TWO of you! I thought there was only one. Well, come in. I'm Thor. Not much space I'm afraid, and I hope you like cats. Willoughby down there is very friendly but he doesn't take kindly to sauciness or cheek."

We looked past Thor to a small, very plump sofa at the end of the room where an enormous tabby cat lay stretched out along the back. He regarded us with the usual disdain. The big green eyes never blinked.

"So, which one's the comedian?"

This cat could speak Dog! How weird. But Gertrude didn't notice and, always quick to take offense, bristled.

"What do you mean?"

"Well, I'd heard on Cat's Whisker that one of you pugs was gifted at making people laugh. I was looking forward to that."

Don't know how the news had spread, but in one of my earlier blogs I described how Gertrude had attempted to steal my part in the Christmas Panto at our small local theatre. It was an accident of mistaken identity that she got involved and she caused total chaos, but did make people howl with laughter. She never stops talking about it.

"Think Willoughby might be referring to your theatrical triumphs, Gertie."

I tried hard not to growl with irritation.

Gertrude yelped with delight.

"Oh that. Well, it was quite fun. Most people seemed to enjoy it anyway." She sniffed in a rather 'I'm just a humble celeb' kind of way.

The green eyes glittered. "Well, don't try any funny business here, and just remember that I run this boat. So no fighting, be on time for your meals, and don't go ashore without permission. 'Spect you noticed a very strong scent as soon as you arrived? Well, that's 'cos we're right up close to The Zoo."

"The Zoo?" I said. "What's that?"

"It's like a big park for lots of different animals. They come from all over the world and they live there, some in the open, but mostly in cages 'cos some of them are quite dangerous. They're wild animals you see, not like us. We've learnt how to manage humans, but they just want to eat them."

Gertrude looked startled. "Would they want to eat me?"

"Some of them might. You'd make a tasty snack for a lion, I should think."

Thor sniggered. "Oh, Willoughby, stop trying to scare them."

The cat got up, stretched and yawned.

"Just want them to understand that going around here unaccompanied is not wise."

"No chance of that," I said, my voice squeaky with fear.

"Good! Lesson learned then," and he jumped down softly, in spite of his impressive size, and strolled towards the steps that led up to the deck.

"Think I'll go ashore for a stroll. See what's happening."
And with a wave of his tail he leapt up gracefully and
vanished through the cat flap.

Gertrude and I looked at each other.

"Hope we're not staying too long," I said.

"Oh, come on, Toastie. This could be a great adventure."

I looked at her nervously. Her eyes were shining with
mischief.

Bedtime

A quick post before I curl up. I've got to tell you about our walk after supper this evening. Old Deck Shoes and Slippers took us along the path by the water, scary enough in itself, I'm not a good swimmer. But it was the roaring!

"ARRRRH,OOOOUUUMMM! AHHHHOOOOUUM! UHRRRRR, AHRRRRH, UHRRRRR!"

Very loud and deep, and kind of hollow. I can tell you I nearly sicked up my supper as soon as I heard it. It was horrible, like a big paw grabbing my insides. I stuck as close to Slippers as I could.

Of course, Gertrude was all for running ahead as far as her lead would allow, encouraged by Thor who was tripping along on his tiny little paws, not on a lead. She could hardly wait to see what was roaring. I could hear snatches of their conversation that made my ears quiver.

"So can we.............zoo?"

"I go every.............want to.............me."

"Oooooh yes!"

"........go early while Willoughby..........way.......
out at night."

Sounds to me like they're plotting something.

Curiosity gave me the courage to move up a little closer
behind them, just as Thor was saying in a casual way,

"I work at the zoo. I take messages between the
animals."

He looked to see if Gertrude was impressed.

"I can speak all the languages you see."

Gertrude was both impressed and startled.

"What languages? You mean not just Cat and Dog?"

"Oh! That's nothing. I can speak Tiger, rather badly,
don't have the muscle for it, Lion, same thing, Gorilla,
Chimpanzee, Camel, Elephant. And Meerkat, really well.
Then I can manage some basic stuff in the other monkey
languages, some Pig and a bit of Giraffe. The big birds are
difficult, but they're so rude and aggressive it's not worth
bothering with them. And I can't do Reptile at all, but they
don't say much anyway."

He's got to be lying, I thought, could he really know what that roaring was about? I trotted up a bit closer.

"Was that a lion, Thor?"

"No, that was Mira the tiger. She was teasing her mate Simba. He sits on their tree platform for hours gazing hungrily at the dogs scampering by in the park outside the zoo. So she just said, 'Dreaming of the little doggies again are you? Greedy guts.' He calls me Snack. Just a joke, but he enjoys a gossip."

Still don't quite believe it, but I'll have to try and stay awake tonight, in case Gertrude does something stupid.

Early. Before next breakfast.

Of course, I went to sleep didn't I? Woke to find Gertrude gone, Thor's bed empty and Willoughby's unblinking eyes staring at me three inches from my nose. It was scary.

"So, where's your funny friend? Out early isn't she? Thor thinks I don't know he goes to the Zoo every morning, but that doesn't worry me. He knows how to handle himself. He's quick-witted and can always get himself out of trouble with his knack for languages. But I have a feeling that that Gertrude is a problem. Reckless, fearless and stupid. It's a bad mix."

This is one smart cat I thought, so respectfully stammered,

"W-w-w-w what, what should we do?"

"Well, I suppose we should go and look for them. Are you up for that? We'll have to do it before our human chums wake up or there'll be a horrible fuss."

I would rather have stayed safely in bed, but I was too scared of Willoughby to refuse. We left by the cat flap, a bit of a squash for me but I went first and Willoughby pushed me through. He is very strong.

"Come on, we'll visit the meerkats first, I can almost understand them. They're tremendous gossips so Thor always goes to them first."

We scampered quickly along the bank and then Willoughby plunged into the bushes. He has his own secret way into the zoo, which of course I can't reveal.

We passed some horribly big birds with scary feathered trousers, huge beaks and fierce, cruel eyes. They were hunched on the branches of leafless trees. They screamed at us and I ran on quickly.

Finally, we stopped in front of a railing and Willoughby gave a weird chirpy yowl, sort of a mixture of Dog, and something else. Immediately three bright little pointy faces appeared from inside a sandy hillock and, before you could say Ears and Tails, transformed into three tall, skinny little chaps sitting bolt upright in front of us.

Willoughby said something and they chirruped back.

"Prrrrrrrup, prup prrrrruuuup prp. Prrrruup prrup prrrrrruuuuuup."

The cat snorted and turned to me.

"We've only just missed them. Come on."

I would have liked to stay and hear more from these cheerful creatures. I could tell from the alert way they listened that they didn't miss much. Another chirrup followed us as Willoughby set off quickly down a narrow path.

"Huh! So they're heading for the monkeys are they? But which ones? There's lots of different types, so that's not much help."

I had a quick "look around" with my nose and yelped,

"Willoughby! They went this way, I've picked up the scent...... and there's somebody with them."

"I know that, stupid! We're just taking a short cut, because the meerkats also told me they'd heard that a new gorilla was arriving this morning, which means everyone will be restless and excited. Things could get lively." He paused, puzzled. "Who can they be with?"

With that, he plunged into some bushes and vanished from sight. I followed as quickly as I could but he was nowhere to be seen. I stood still, gulping with fear. If I barked would he come back, or would something else find me? I put my nose to the ground and followed his scent, but it suddenly stopped. My heart froze. Had somebody pounced and eaten him? No, don't be silly I said to myself. There'd have been a fight, or at least a squeal.

There were so many unfamiliar smells it was hard to know what to follow. I was just standing there, wondering what to do, when something big came out of the tree above me and landed softly at my side. I nearly died of fright..... It was Willoughby!

"Where did you go?" I snapped. He grinned mischievously.

"Thought I'd deserted you?" He gave a low, yowlly laugh, "Marrough-ough-ough-ough! Just thought I'd nip up this tree and take a quick look and see what's happening. We don't want to walk into any trouble when we could have avoided it, do we? Come on, the coast's clear."

But it wasn't. A moment later there was a blood-curdling scream.

"AAAAAAAAAAaaaaaaahhhhh."

And someone else dropped from the tree and a thin hand seized the back of my neck.

"Eeeyipe! Yipe!" I squealed in a voice I hardly recognised. The scent of whatever had grabbed me was so overpowering it almost choked me.

"Willoughby! Help!" I croaked. But there was no answer. My captor now set off at speed through the bushes, half carrying and half dragging me by the scruff of my neck.

"Please don't eat me, I'm just a friendly pug."

But of course whatever it was didn't understand and just went on screaming,

"AAAAAaaahh, EEEEeehhh, aaaahheEEEEH!"

I kept hoping this was just a nightmare and that I'd wake up in my nice warm bed. I thought I heard someone else talking, but the scream was so close to my ear that I couldn't make out what it was.

Finally, we broke free of the bushes and I was then dragged along a path overhung by trees. My heart was pounding. Was I being taken back to a cage to be eaten for breakfast?

Suddenly, to my astonishment, we rounded a corner and I was dumped like an old handbag in front of Thor and Gertrude who were talking to two creatures up in a tree.

I should have guessed Gertrude had something to do with this horror. She gaped in amazement and then yelped with laughter.

"Dear me, Toastie, you look like you've been dragged through a hedge backwards."

"I have been," I barked furiously, "and I suppose I have you to thank for it."

"Why me? I didn't ask you to follow us. I knew you'd only try and spoil things."

"It wasn't me who was worried, it was Willoughby. He dragged me out of bed to look for you."

The mention of the powerful cat got Thor's attention. He stopped talking to his two friends in the tree and whirled round to face me.

"Willoughby?" He sounded cross. "Where is he? I thought he was with you. How did he know we were here anyway?"

"He told me he's always known that you come here every morning. He's not worried about you, he's worried about Gertrude, specially when he heard a new gorilla is arriving today. There will be a lot of keepers about."

"Yes, yes, yes," Thor said impatiently.

I could see he was flustered.

"We know about that, but where is Willoughby now?"

He turned back to his friends in the tree.

"These are my monkey chums by the way. They're gibbons. Don't they have beautiful voices?"

I didn't think so, especially not at close quarters, but I said nothing. The two long-limbed creatures in the tree had now been joined by my captor who was grinning at me as if nothing had happened. Thor let out a weird string of high-pitched screams, and a lively conversation followed.

Then he turned to us and said,

"I asked Chubbs to bring you both here, but gently and politely, not like a packed lunch." He looked crossly at Chubbs. "But he gets over excited. He just told me that he did introduce himself and explained where he was taking you, but you didn't reply. So he grabbed you and when he looked round Willoughby had vanished. Very annoying."

"But how did you know we were here?"

I was getting more and more confused.

"I heard one of the vultures telling a pair of eagles that two strangers were in the zoo, and that one was a scrappy little dog with a flat face like a monkey, just like the other one. So I knew it must be you."

"Just a minute," Gertrude said. "I don't like that!"

"Well, well, I warned you that the big birds could be rude. No point in getting upset."

Before we had time to reply, Chubbs gave one massive scream.

"Waaaaaaaaaaaaaahhhhh EEEEEEEEEEHHHHHH!"

35

My heart nearly jumped out of my mouth, but Thor, cool as anything, was just listening attentively.

"Come on, we'd better hide quickly. There are two keepers just round the corner."

With that he ran swiftly back down the path and into the bushes. We didn't need telling what to do. Gertrude got to safety before Thor. The gibbons had vanished. Two men rounded the corner, moving quickly. They were looking around, their eyes darting everywhere. I hoped they weren't looking for us. All three of us picked up their scent, it was thick with anxiety. We stayed very still. We could hear people shouting. Thor was fidgety with irritation.

"If only I could understand Human, but it's so difficult and they speak so fast. We'll just have to use our noses."

"And your eyes, but you've been too busy showing off, my little friend, haven't you? Marrrough-ough-ough-ough."

Willoughby's familiar soft, yowlly laugh was suddenly right behind us. How can he creep up so silently? Thor jumped and, pretending he hadn't, spun round to face the cat.

"What do you mean? What have we missed?"

"Well, when I was up the tree, moments before your monkey friend scared Miss Toast half witless, I could see something was going on near the entrance. Looked like there was a lot of excitement happening round a big truck. You must have noticed how restless everyone is. Even the penguins were keeping out of sight under the water. I saw two or three of them talking to a heron, but suddenly they all dived. Sorry I had to leave you, Miss Toast, but it all happened too quickly for me to do anything. I did tell you I was right behind you and would sort it, but when I saw you being taken to Thor, I knew you'd be OK, so I went to find out what was going down."

"So tell us. What did you see?" Gertrude was on fire with curiosity.

The big tabby shifted uneasily.

"Well, I got as near as I could without being seen. Lucky that Human noses are so useless, all the animals nearby knew where I was. Anyway, I could just see what looked like a very, very big monkey, with dark fur but grey on his back. He's in a cage on the back of a big truck. He looked sleepy and kind of sad, poor thing. They're coming in this direction."

"That'll be the new gorilla, we're right on the edge of his new home," Thor said, trying to show he was still boss.

"Maybe we should move away," I said in a small voice.

"No! No! No! I want to see him," squealed Gertrude. She was capering backwards and forwards on her hind legs with excitement.

"Quiet everyone. Nobody move a muscle. Here they come."

Nobody was going to disobey Willoughby, so we all shut up. I stayed very still and wondered if I'd ever have my breakfast.

We could hear the truck's engine now, and then round the corner it came, moving slowly. We watched through the pale fuzz of new leaves as it crept towards us, two men talking gently to whoever was in the cage. It passed really close to us and there, inside, sat a massive animal with hands, not paws, and feet quite like a human's. It had a huge face with small sad eyes. A tear was crawling down one leathery cheek.

Gertrude gave a little cry and lunged forward. The big gorilla catching sight of the movement swung its head round and its eyes settled on Gertrude.

"Ahhhgrrrrrrraaah!" A rumbling cry from deep inside trickled from his throat. The truck stopped while they opened the doors to his new home. Taking advantage of the keepers' backs being turned, Thor made a similar sound only much, much smaller. The gorilla, considerably surprised, looked round to see who had spoken. When he finally realised it was a tiny ball of ginger fluff on thin legs he looked somewhat shaken, but nevertheless answered politely with another series of rumbles.

Darting back out of sight, Thor turned to us proudly.

"He says he's lonely and fed-up and that this doesn't look any better than the last zoo he was in. I told him he had three female gorillas waiting to make him welcome, and he said, 'Oh, they'll only squabble and nag.' I think he's just tired after a long journey. His name's Arthur by the way, but he says his mother named him Wahalah, so I think that's what we should call him."

The men were now helping him out of the truck and were about to lead him into his new kingdom, when Gertrude suddenly shot forward.

"I think I'll just go and cheer him up."

All of us tried to stop her, but she was too quick. Willoughby yowled with rage.

"I just knew she was going to cause trouble."

We watched helplessly as Gertrude nipped through the gate and, before the men could grab her, there she was sitting on her hind legs in front of Wahalah, her flat little face turned up to his.

With a cry of joy the great beast leant forward and with one huge hand scooped Gertrude up.

He then cradled her like a baby, stroking her face and nibbling softly at her ears.

"Gwuuurrrck. Uummgwurrck!"

"What did he say?" Willoughby nudged Thor.

"He said, 'Thank you, thank you. Just the little friend I wanted.'"

I looked doubtful. "But he looks like he might eat her."

"No, no, no. Gorillas eat leaves and twigs." Thor spoke in his best teacher voice.

"But how can we get her away from him?" I was feeling very anxious, knowing how angry Slippers would be if anything bad happened to her.

Thor thought for a moment, then coming close to me he whispered, "What did she do to make people laugh?"

"She dressed up and danced. It really was quite funny."

"Danced, eh? I've got an idea."

Thor's tiny high-pitched voice let out a stream of "Ummguuwurrcks" and the gorilla turned and listened with interest, then answered slowly,

"Nnggwuurrk, gwuurrk."

"What's going on?" Willoughby was getting impatient. He didn't like not being in charge.

"I told Wahalah that Gertrude just popped in to cheer him up with a bit of entertainment, but that she'll have to go afterwards. He has agreed because he's very curious to see what she does." Then he raised his voice again and called to Gertrude.

"Gertrude! Wahalah wants to see you dance. Make it really special and he'll be happy to let you go. OK?"

Gertrude nodded as best she could. Wahalah was holding her rather tightly.

Then we watched as he tenderly put her on the ground and sat back for his promised entertainment. The keepers meanwhile had been handed long poles with a net on the end and obviously had every intention of capturing Gertrude. But when they saw her start her dance, they were as entranced as the gorilla. Leaping onto her hind-legs she capered back and forth, waving her front paws, twirling around. She did two back flips and a somersault, dancing and spinning in a wide circle in front of the delighted Wahalah. During her dance, she grabbed a juicy looking shoot from a nearby bush then holding this in her mouth she came to a dazzling finish standing on her front paws. We all thought this must be the end, but no, she paused a moment, to balance carefully. Then, amazingly, lifted one paw off the ground, paused for effect, then flipped onto her hind legs and presented the juicy looking shoot to the astonished gorilla.

"GWUUURRCK NNGWUUURRK GWUUURRCK. OOOUUMMGWURRRK, OOUUMMMGGH."

Wahalah, looking a lot more cheerful, bent forward and a huge hand patted Gertrude on the head. He then gratefully took the shoot and ate it immediately.

"Did he like her dance?" I asked quite anxiously.

"Of course he did. He just said thank you didn't he?"

"Well, I don't know. You're the one who speaks Gorilla."

Thor looked at me, his eyes sparkling. "He loved it. He's very flattered and he wants her to come back tomorrow. What a triumph!" Then, turning to Gertrude, he barked,

"Come on, Gertrude. You'd better get out before the men stop laughing."

The men were stamping their feet and slapping their thighs they were laughing so hard, but for once in her life Gertrude acted sensibly. Bowing low to Wahalah, she ran out of the still open gate before they knew what had happened. She and Thor ran towards the bushes where Willoughby and I had kept out of sight, and the four of us rushed back towards the meerkats. We could hear the men shouting, but Wahalah covered our escape with a good deal of noise and some very impressive chest beating, so they had to pay attention to him and make sure he was safely locked inside his new home.

We roared past the vultures and eagles who squawked in a very unpleasant way.

"WEEOOEEEOOWEERRUHHHH."

They ruffled their feathers, their angry beaks jutting forward. I looked away quickly. I didn't ask what they had said.

" They're just jealous," Thor said mysteriously.

The meerkats were waiting, on tiptoe with excitement, their inquisitive little faces eager for news. A chorus of chirruped enquiry greeted Thor. He answered briefly and we sped on, followed by chirrups of disappointment.

"I'll have to tell them all about it tomorrow morning."

Finally we were back on the canal bank and were just about to rush onto the boat when Willoughby stopped us.

"I'll go in first and see what's happening. We've been out a very long time and our human chums might not be too happy. A lot of purring might fix it, they love that. You three wait here."

None of us fancied arguing with the huge cat, so we stayed where we were.

I could see this didn't please Thor, but the tabby had already jumped up and vanished through the cat flap. We waited to see if he'd come back to tell us if we'd been missed. But he didn't.

"Well, we better get it over with, come on."

With that, Thor leapt onto the deck and pushed his way through the flap. There was a shout of greeting, then a lot more shouting. The door flew open and there was Old Deck Shoes, with Slippers right behind her. They looked at our guilty faces and roared with laughter. They shook their fingers at us, still laughing, and held the door open for us to go in. We all wagged our tails as hard as we could and jumped up and licked the hands of our friends.

I don't think we'd have been made so welcome if they knew what we'd been up to. But we didn't spend too much time worrying about that as we'd spotted our breakfast bowls. My goodness we were hungry and moments later we had our noses down, gratefully gulping back our food. Gertrude carefully licked every trace of breakfast from her bowl, then stood back and looked greedily at what was left of mine.

"How long are we staying, Toastie?" she said, moving closer.

I finished every last bit of food before answering.

"Don't know, Gertie. I'd be happy to go home now."

Gertrude looked away dreamily.

"Well, I'd like to stay here for ever and go to the zoo every day and play with Wahalah. I'd make Thor teach me the languages so I could talk to everyone. How much fun would that be?"

"Too much excitement for me I'm afraid. I'm exhausted."

Slippers and Old Deck Shoes were still shovelling in the toast and coffee, talking and laughing loudly. Usually I would have jumped up, put a paw on Slippers' knee and looked hopeful. I like a bit of toast and marmalade. But instead I headed for a cosy corner and curled up on the cushions. As I drifted off to sleep, the events of the morning swam before my eyes. Had it all really happened? Had Gertie danced to amuse a gorilla? Willoughby, who was once again in his favourite place stretched along the back of the sofa, looked across at me and winked. But I might have imagined that.

"Marrraough-augh-augh-augh."

I hardly heard his yowlly laugh. The next second I was fast asleep.

Much Later

CAKE! I COULD SMELL CAKE! It woke me up.

What's happening? Where am I? It took me a moment to work it out. I must have been asleep for ages.

It seemed I was alone on the boat, but the door was open and I could hear Slippers and Old Deck Shoes talking outside. I rushed up onto the deck and there they were. They'd taken chairs out and were sitting on the bank. Between them was a small table and on it a large, iced cake, a big teapot and two mugs.

I called to Slippers who got up and lifted me off the boat, putting me on the grass next to her chair. I watched hungrily as the cake was cut and she took a huge piece. I knew she wouldn't give me any, but I stayed watchful in case of crumbs. No sign of Gertrude and Thor, but I could hear Gertie shouting and Thor's squeaky voice joining in, but they were too far away to make out what they were saying. I wished I was a bit more daring and could run off and join them. Just then Willoughby came strolling along the path. He brushed affectionately against Old Deck Shoes' legs, purring loudly, and was given a saucer of milk as a reward.

He finished it quickly, then, licking his lips and carefully cleaning his whiskers with a paw, turned to me and grinned.

"Must say your friend really did make me laugh. What a show!"

"Admired her pluck, too. Took a lot of courage to do that."

I had to agree, even though his comments made me feel even more of a wimp. He sat next to me and carried on his routine with the whiskers. Cats take a lot of trouble with their appearance. When he'd finally finished he said thoughtfully,

"Never seen Thor so impressed with another dog, and of course he laps up Gertrude's admiration. They're suddenly the best of friends. Don't like it. He might encourage her in more mad schemes."

With that he jumped on board and vanished inside. I sat waiting for a few cake crumbs and wished we could go home. The tea things went in and glasses of something pink came out before Thor came trotting back down the path. He was on his own. Gertrude's absence caused a huge fuss. Slippers didn't like it and called and called her, but she didn't appear. Thor made a sniggery sound and said,

"They needn't worry, she's not far away. She's just talking to a Jack Russell from one of the other boats. He's very interested in hearing about her adventures with Wahalah. She wants to go into the zoo again, but I told her she couldn't, not with all the people around."

"Wish you could tell Slippers that."

"So do I, Miss Toast, so do I."

His casual attitude made me cross. Slippers had wandered along the path still calling Gertie's name, so Old Deck Shoes cleared everything back on board and joined her in the search. I stuck close to their heels and kept track of Gertrude's scent.

It took us to a much wider bit of water with lots of boats, but no sign of Gertie or a Jack Russell. I ran round following in her paw prints but she seemed to be going in circles so it wasn't easy to work out where she'd gone. I'd almost given up when I picked up her scent leading to Willoughby's secret entry to the zoo. Oh no! She couldn't be so stupid surely? I ran back to Slippers and tried to explain, but she couldn't understand and just got cross.

This decided me. I'd have to go and look for Gertrude myself.

It meant missing supper. With a heavy heart I plunged into the bushes, picked up the scent and moved forward as quietly as I could. It was getting late so I supposed all the people would have gone home, but I had to be careful. I hoped Gertrude would have headed for the meerkats as Willoughby had done, but she hadn't. I came out of the bushes somewhere we hadn't been that morning and was shocked to see some striped horses. Was I dreaming? Then some enormous animals with very, very long necks and smart coats patterned with squares.

They saw me and started making weird noises that they obviously thought I'd understand. Some of Thor's friends I suppose. I ran past them but seemed to have lost Gertie's scent. I couldn't see anything familiar and feared I was lost.

Suddenly I heard human voices close by. I had to find somewhere to hide, but I was in the open with no handy bushes to run to. I looked around frantically and saw an open door. Hooray! I could hide in there until they'd gone by. I rushed in and was instantly overwhelmed with a strong cat-like scent. Oh! This was a big mistake, I thought. I didn't realise then just how big a mistake it was.

Instead of walking by, the keepers came straight up to the door, shouted something through it, waited, and then slammed it shut. I was trapped, and I didn't know with what.

I crept forward cautiously. One room led to two bigger ones. At the end of one of these was a tunnel with a barred gate across one end, so I squeezed through the bars and found myself in yet another room with an open door on the far side.

I was relieved to see leaves and grasses outside, so I ran across, and leaping gratefully into the tall grass, dashed forward into some jungly plants. I had no idea where I was and was just looking around to get my bearings when to my horror I heard a familiar growling roar closer than was comfortable.

"GGRRRRUUUURHHHUUUURHOOOM."

The TIGERS! I froze. My heart felt as if it would leap out of my mouth. I looked around desperately and to my horror I realised I had got myself inside their jungly home. Worse, the roar was coming from somewhere above me. The sun had almost gone now and all the animals in the zoo were calling to each other. What were they saying? 'Enjoy your supper, tigers. That little dog should make a tender, tasty meal?'

I couldn't help it, I screamed with fright. A bad idea as this only attracted the attention of the huge beasts, who I could now see up on their favourite tree platform watching the dogs on the path outside the zoo. I could hear them padding softly across the logs overhead as they came to see what had screamed. The next minute, two pairs of golden eyes were looking straight down at me.

They both licked their lips and headed to the tree trunks that led down to the ground. There was a lot of pushing and squabbling about which of them would go first.

I think that saved my life, because at that moment Gertrude appeared on the other side of the glass where the public could view the tigers. She was running backwards and forwards on her hind legs. The tigers suddenly noticed her and their eyes widened with surprise. They looked down to where they'd last seen me, but I'd quickly hidden myself. Then they looked back at Gertrude who was by now standing upside-down on one paw. I could see from my hiding place that they didn't like this. Their ears went back and they had to sit down. They must have been wondering how the tasty meal they'd spotted was now teasing them from the other side of the glass!

Gertrude was barking as loudly as she could, and I suddenly realised she was shouting at me. My fear had almost made me deaf.

"Toastie! Get back to the door fast as you can. Run through to the front and wait there. A keeper is on his way with his arms full of straw. Rush out as soon as he opens the door and hide. Me and Thor will come and find you."

I was about to obey her instructions when I saw Thor bound into view. I could hear him start to talk to the tigers and could see they looked very attentive, but I didn't wait to see what would happen. Dashing back to the door, I rushed in, squeezed through the gate, ran through the tunnel and the gloomy rooms, and waited panting by the door to the outside. My mouth was dry as a bone. The lock turned and the keeper appeared in the doorway. The bundle of straw was so enormous he could hardly see over it, so he didn't see me dart through to freedom and safety.

Shaking from ears to tail I ran to the nearest hiding place, round the side of a nearby building and lay down. I could sense other animals staring at me from their cages, all talking at once, and saw the keeper come out again and firmly lock the door behind him. It all felt like a dream and I have no idea how long I was there.

"You alright, Toastie? You don't look too good. We'd better get you out of here fast."

It was Gertrude, and behind her was Thor, as usual looking very pleased with himself. I wagged my tail. I've never been so glad to see another two dogs in my life. I staggered to my paws and went and licked their noses.

"Come on, Miss T. Let's get back to the boat before anyone finds us here."

Thor sounded excited. He went another secret way back and before we knew it we were on the bank. The light was fading fast and a wind had sprung up. Lamps were being lit in the boats which moved, creaking, on the water. Before we got back to our one, Thor suddenly made a sniggery sound and said,

"Did you hear that cheering, Toastie? Everyone was very impressed. What a triumph!"

I was puzzled. "Triumph for whom?"

"For the three of us of course."

"Why?"

"For teasing the tigers. They're such divas. It was brilliant. I told them that Gertie is a magic dog who can appear in two places at once. Bless them, they believed it. Simple souls, tigers. Big dinners, sleep, being looked at by admiring people, that they understand. But a doggie snack being in two places at once and teasing them by standing on one paw made their stripes crawl."

Thor and Gertrude danced about each other, delighted at their cleverness.

"Tell Toastie about the gorilla. That's the best bit."

I've never seen Gertrude so happy. Thor stopped springing up and down and turned to me.

"Oh, yes. This really annoyed them. I told them that Gertrude was the best and most treasured friend of Wahalah, the new gorilla, and that it would make him very cross if anything bad happened to her. They didn't like it, but they believed that too."

"Well, it's true." Gertrude looked defiant. "I went back to see him, Toastie, to make sure he'd settled in, you know. He was delighted, and invited his three lady friends, who he finds he likes very much, to join him while I did another dance. I added more somersaults this time. It was pretty impressive, Thor, wasn't it?

Thor agreed.

" But, Toastie, what were you doing in the tiger's jungly home?"

"Looking for YOU. Slippers was worried and was calling and calling and I just knew you must have gone back to see Wahalah again, so I followed your scent but got lost. I got into the tiger's jungly home by mistake when I heard some keepers coming and needed a hiding place. It would have been fine. I was just inside the door and meant to leave as soon as they went by, but they slammed it shut. I hoped I could get out the other side of the rooms but it led straight into the jungly bit. I'll never be able to thank you enough for rescuing me, Gertie."

"Oh, come on, Toastie, I wouldn't let you become a tiger snack. I ran, fast as I could as soon as Thor told me that the camels had spotted you in a very dangerous place. I knew if I could distract the tigers it would give you the time to escape and Thor the chance to stop them from eating you."

The thought of that made me feel quite faint. I even forgot how hungry I was. I soon remembered when I got back to the boat though. Our suppers were waiting for us, and Old Deck Shoes and Slippers were so relieved to see us they weren't even cross. We got our noses down straight away. Willoughby was watching us from the back of the sofa. He waited till we'd finished then said softly,

"Glad to see you safely back here, Miss Toast. I went to see the Meerkats and they told me they'd heard you'd been eaten by the tigers. They'd also heard that Gertrude had been kidnapped by the gorilla and was being used as a football by his lady friends. But as I said before, they are terrible gossips and like their stories sensational, so I didn't take much notice. Think I misjudged Gertrude though. She may be stupid, but she's got a lot of courage. You really would have been toast without her!"

Pleased with his little joke, he sat up, sniffed, and started grooming his whiskers again.

"It's been fun, but I shan't be sorry to see you two go home tomorrow. I like my peace and quiet on this boat."

Gertrude looked up sharply.

"Go home! Are we going home? But I want to stay here."

" Well, I watched the bags being packed. So I think it's goodbye."

Gertrude went very quiet and sulked. I'd better keep an eye on her.

Next Breakfast

I slept like a log and woke to find Thor and Gertrude's beds empty. OH, NO! NOT AGAIN! Slippers was still asleep, so I pottered out on deck. Willoughby was on the bank doing his early morning face and whisker cleaning.

" Morning, Miss T. Don't panic about those two rascals. I told Thor that if he promised to get her back quickly, he could take Gertrude to say goodbye to Wahalah."

"Well, we can only hope that he keeps his promise."

Just then, a little Jack Russell came trotting jauntily along the bank.

"Hi, Willoughby. Is Gertrude about?"

"No, Sam, she's in the zoo with Thor."

"Oh, pity, I was going to take her round the boats further along the canal and introduce her to some of the dogs up there. They're a rowdy bunch but good-natured."

"Well, that'll have to wait till her next visit, if there is one, that is. Gertrude, and Miss Toast there," he waved a paw in my direction, "are off home today."

Sam turned and looked at me.

"Hello! You must be the pug Gertrude went to rescue. Brilliant wasn't it?"

"It certainly was. Nice to meet you, Sam. Hey! Here they come."

We all looked down the bank and there were Gertrude and Thor running joyfully towards us. Gertrude was breathless with excitement.

"Wahalah was terribly disappointed that I have to go. I had to do a farewell dance, and all the other animals got as close as they could, it was TERRIFIC. Hi, Sam. Good of you to come and say goodbye. What a wonderful time we've all had."

Willoughby looked at me and gave his soft, yowlly chuckle.

"Bit of a scary time for Miss Toast I think."

Gertrude looked surprised.

"Oh, come on, Toastie. You must admit it's been the best adventure we've ever had."

I thought about this all the way home in Slippers' smelly old car. I suppose, although I spent a lot of the time half scared to death, without Gertrude it might have been quite a dull weekend.

We got home to find Teddy and Shiny Shoes waiting at the gate.

"Have a good time?" Teddy asked doubtfully.

"The best time EVER. Didn't we, Toastie?"

Gertrude's eyes were shining, and, remembering her fearless rescue – I mean I owed her my life – I turned to Teddy with a grin and giving Gertie a lick, I said,

"We certainly did! It's the most exciting weekend I've ever had."

THE END